Hidden

A DRAGONS OF THE CROSSROADS PREQUEL

LORI SALTIS

VAGABOND TALES

To Brian Mathis, my dear friend and fellow wanderer. You left this world too soon.

Lost

Dear Mom,

This feels stupid, but I don't know what else to do. I need to talk to you.

I need to see you!

I can't believe I won't ever see you again. It doesn't feel real. I know you're dead, but I still can't believe it. As long as I can write to you, maybe it doesn't have to be real.

Dad and the twins came back from London and you weren't with them. I asked where you were and why you stayed behind, and they wouldn't answer. Dad had turned to stone and George was like a whipped dog, while Mike was cold and mean to everyone but me.

I tried calling you about a hundred times, but you didn't answer. Finally, Mike sat me down and told me you'd died in battle saving someone's life, but he won't say why you fought or who you saved. Dad made him and George swear an oath to keep every-

thing that happened in London hidden. I begged and even screamed, but all he said was, "Look, Cat, Dad's the Dragon Son. If he wants something hidden, it stays hidden."

I've set up a shrine for you in the alcove because no one else will. I've left fruit, lit incense and candles, and prayed as hard as I could. The only thing I haven't done is cry, not even at your funeral. I can't, not until I know how you died.

I set down my journal and rub my forehead. My head hasn't stopped aching since Dad and my brothers returned to San Francisco. I'm sitting at the top of the stairs, staring down into the black hole that's become our home. Dad wakes up around noon and heads straight for Marshes, the Crossroads bar in Chinatown, and doesn't come home until it closes. Whenever I try talking to him, he waves me away. Mike and George are usually gone, too, except for this morning. Thumping and scraping sounds have been coming from below for almost half-an-hour. Are they fighting? Rearranging the furniture? It sounds more like that, but why?

"Motherfucker," Mike shouts.

I jump to my feet, clutching my journal to my chest.

"I don't care what Mother says or does. This is on you."

I grimace, but don't head downstairs because that's nothing I need to get involved with. Their mother, Dad's First Wife, has always been a bone of contention between them. When he left her to be with my mother, he took Mike with them to San Francisco, but left George behind in Hong Kong. I don't know how anyone thought that was a good idea, splitting up twins. They're fraternal, not identical, but still. It's been hardest on George. He was born two minutes after Mike. Two minutes between him and being the Dragon Son's Heir and head of the Crossroads. They spent their summers together, one month here and two months there, but that's not enough time to get close, especially with parents who hate each other.

How could Dad have been so selfish? Is it that selfishness now that's allowing him to drink away his grief while I suffer alone in silence?

I sit back down and lean against the wall, resting my head against its cold, smooth surface. I close my eyes and think about the last time Mom and I sparred. It was an early Saturday morning and she'd driven us to a remote beach on the Marin coast. It was low tide, but the sand was still wet and clumps of seaweed lingered, their smell growing stronger as the sun pierced the fog. I'd finished learning the movements for the Phoenix Defeats Dragon sword form more than a year ago, but Mom continued drilling the variations into me. Only women in the Two Dragon Clan are taught this form and its secrets of harnessing yin to defeat yang energy, and Mom was an expert.

I take after Dad in height, so I'm way taller than her, but I still felt like a child when she set down her sword and came behind me, placing her hands over mine and demonstrating how to swing the sword.

"You're still slicing. Don't slice. Flow. Feel the flow of your opponent's energy. That's how you'll anticipate his every move, match and overcome them."

Flow. I need to flow. But how the hell can I flow when I don't know who my enemy is or what I'm fighting against?

Arguing voices float up from below, but it's not my brothers this time. They're coming from the ground floor. It's Peter Chan, head of security, and a woman... I don't recognize her voice. Both are speaking Cantonese, but my mind is too weary to translate. With a sigh, I heave myself up and head downstairs.

We live in the *kongsi*, the San Francisco headquarters of the Two Dragon Clan. The top floor is reserved for the Dragon Son and his family, while the second floor is for his adult offspring, like Mike and George. The ground and first floors are for general clan usage. The *kongsi* is in Joseph Alley on the outer fringes of Chinatown and nowhere near any hotels or shops. The entrance, though, is decorated with an ornate awning that attracts the occasional tourist.

The front door is wide open and several men are hauling in a bunch of luggage. A young woman is standing beside the security desk, hands on hips, her chin lifted so her arrogant glare can pierce any opposition. She's wearing a bright red dress and matching heels, and her long hair has red highlights and thick curls. As I get closer, I see she isn't young and I wonder if she realizes her thick makeup only works at a distance.

I roll my eyes. I'm not in the mood, but I'll be nice and set her straight. "Hi. Can I help you?"

Her nostrils flare. She looks me up and down like I'm a homeless person reeking of urine. "You're The Girl."

Oh my god. It's Tiffany. My skin crawls. What the hell is she doing here?

She turns to Peter Chan and snaps her fingers. "Where are my sons?"

Holy shit. I have to get her out of here, but how? Dad. I turn and run upstairs.

As expected, he's sprawled across the bed, clutching Mom's pillow to his chest, sleeping it off. In the dim light, with the curtains drawn and his eyes closed, he looks so young, like a sorrowful child. Then I yank open the curtains and harsh daylight etches lines on his face that hadn't been there before Mom died.

"Dad? Dad." I repeat that several more times before shaking him.

He groans as if in pain before blinking open red-rimmed eyes. They fill with tears as he stares at me and whispers, "You look so much like her."

I don't. I look like him. Everyone says so. Why is he acting this way? A commotion comes from the stairs, voices arguing and stomping feet. Is she coming up here? "Dad, you have to wake up. Tiffany is here."

"What?" He frowns as if I'd told a bad joke. "What do you mean she's here?"

"She's here, in the *kongsi*. Tiffany. Your First Wife. I think she's coming upstairs to see you."

Dad rolls into a sitting position and sways before putting his head between his knees to dry heave. I step back, my stomach twisting. What happened to my brave father who faced any adversary with a devilish smirk?

Finally, he stands. He's wearing only boxers and a stained white T-shirt, but at this point, I don't care. I follow as he staggers out of his room. Down the hall, Tiffany is stepping out the elevator, accompanied by the twins. The guards are hauling her luggage to the top of the stairs. Dad stops and straightens as his blurry face sharpens with fury. He strides over and starts kicking her suitcases downstairs. Each kick widens my smile. I almost want to hug Tiffany for waking him up.

The guards flinch, but she doesn't. She stands there like a high-fashion model in a fixed pose, her lips moving as she mutters something under her breath. Mike leans against the wall with his arms folded and face frozen. Only George tries to intervene, waving his arms at each kick and saying, "Dad, stop. It's not helping."

After the final bag goes sailing downstairs, Dad turns to George, shakes his fist and shouts, "Why is she here?"

George holds up his hands. "I didn't ask her."

Tiffany squeaks out a snort. "I'm here because I'm the Dragon Son's wife."

My heart lifts as Dad's smirk returns. He laughs before looking at her with stone cold eyes. "My wife is dead. You're nothing to me."

"I am the First Wife of the Dragon Son and mother of your sons. No one has taken my place, dead or alive."

My heart starts pounding because, as much as my parents tried to protect me from it, I know what she said is true. Dad never divorced Tiffany because he couldn't, not without alienating her family. So, he made Mom his Second Wife, like back in the day, to keep the peace in the clan.

"You're nothing to me," Dad repeats before shouting, "Get out!"

"You can't make me leave." Tiffany reaches into her enormous purse, pulls out a makeup compact and starts checking her face in the mirror. As she does, she starts muttering again.

I chew my lip, waiting, praying, but Dad's face drains of emotion. Even his voice sounds weaker as he states, "You set foot on this floor again, I'll push you down the stairs and make sure you're dead by the time you reach bottom."

My mouth hangs open as I watch him turn and stagger back to his room. No. No! He was supposed to kick her out and go back to being his old self. Why is he letting her stay? She hates Mom and me. She's the reason I've never been allowed to train at the clan's main compound on Chisel Knife Mountain in Hong Kong.

Tiffany's face pinches with disgust. She snaps her fingers at the guards. "Take my things to the master bedroom on the second floor."

The guards turn blank faces to my brothers. Mike peels himself off the wall and motions them to follow him downstairs. George holds out his arm to his mother and escorts her into the elevator. As the door closes behind them, I realize I'm not alone. A girl about my age is tucked into a doorway. She steps out and stands before me.

"Hi. I'm Leung Si Man," she says in Cantonese, before switching to English, "You can call me Sylvia." Her hands smooth nonexistent wrinkles from her dress. She's dressed in the same mold as Tiffany, though in a more subdued blue. Even her hair has the same red highlights and thick curls. "I'm George's fiancé."

I blink several times before saying, "What? I didn't know George was engaged."

Her eyes go hard and narrow in a way that gives me the creeps, despite her sweet voice. "Actually, I was Michael's fiancé. We've been betrothed since we were children. Then, last year, Head Elder decided he wanted the Dragon Son's Heir to marry his daughter, Michelle, who was betrothed to George. Our parents came to an agreement and we were..." She bites her lip as if about to say an offensive word. "Switched."

I shake my head. "Dad said he'd never arrange marriages for us, that we're free to choose for ourselves."

"Your stepmother arranged their marriages," says Sylvia, "not the Dragon Son."

"She's not my stepmother. And I can't believe my brothers agreed to that."

"George agreed. Michael didn't."

"When is the wedding?"

"The middle of August. I don't know the exact date. No one tells me anything."

I sit on the stairs and cradle my spinning head. I know why Tiffany is doing this. To show everyone that she's the Dragon Son's true wife and Mom was nothing. Not even someone worth mourning. If she held the wedding banquet in Hong Kong, she would still seem the unwanted, exiled First Wife. In San Francisco, at a huge occasion, she's forcing everyone to acknowledge her position.

Sylvia settles beside me, her legs primly folded at an angle as she smooths her dress again. "I'm sorry about your mother. This really wasn't my idea. I hope we can be friends."

I sigh. I don't want to talk to her or be her friend, but she's right. This isn't her fault. I clear my throat before saying, "I'm Catherine, but you can call me Cat."

"Cat." Her smile makes her look a lot more like a cat than I do. She curls in closer to me and whispers, "I don't want to marry George. Can you talk to Michael for me? Remind him that he was promised to me?"

I blink. Wow. I can see why Tiffany switched Sylvia to George. Of course, she wants her favorite son to marry a manipulative bitch, just like her. I get up and walk away. When I get to my room, I close the door and lean against it. My legs are shaking so bad, I can't walk a step further without collapsing.

I thought my life couldn't get any worse. I was so wrong.

Alone

I'm sitting in a pew at Old Saint Mary's Cathedral. When I was a kid, I thought it was named that because Saint Mary was an old woman. Actually, it's the cathedral that's old, as in, there's a newer, bigger Saint Mary's Cathedral in San Francisco, though that one's kind of old, too. I'm not Catholic, so it's confusing.

Old Saint Mary's has a grand, gothic tower with a Roman numeral clock and a plaque that reads: *Son, Observe the Time and Fly from Evil.*

That's what I'm doing here. Flying from the evil that's become my home. Plus, it's the one place in Chinatown that isn't claimed by either the Crossroads or the gangs. It's dark and peaceful, aside from the tourists, but they tend to be quiet. There's this smell of incense, candle wax, and mildew that comforts me. No one bothers me or asks me to leave. I come here so often, I've started leaving money in the collection box. Sometimes I write in my journal, letters to Mom or rants about how much my life sucks, but that gets tiresome. So, I stare at the stained-glass windows and zone out. I close my eyes and hope people think I'm praying.

My pager beeps. I snatch it out of my purse while silently cursing myself for not turning it off. I stare at the message. It's from Mike.

> where u at

I don't answer. I don't want anyone to know I'm here.

> going 2 SFO want 2 come

I chew my lip. I'm so sick of Chinatown right now. I wouldn't mind leaving, even if it is to go to the airport. I text back.

> ok meet @ dragon gate

I slip out of the pew and thread my way through a tour group whose leader speaks in a hushed tone about the fire that destroyed Old Saint Mary's, and much of San Francisco, after the 1906 earthquake. Maybe that's why I like it here so much. I feel like I barely survived one disaster, only to be engulfed in another.

I hurry across California Street and head past the tourist shops lining Grant Avenue until I reach the Dragon Gate. It's a stone arch that spans the width of the street and marks the official entrance to Chinatown. Two giant stone lions guard either side of the street while a pair of dragons face off atop the pagoda-style roof. Beneath them is a plaque with Chinese characters that read: *All Under Heaven is for the Good of the People.*

Yeah, I'm not feeling that. Nothing good has happened since Mom died and nothing will until that bitch leaves our home.

Mike pulls up in his red Camaro and I hop in. He got this car for his twenty-first birthday, while George got a silver BMW. Those two in a nutshell. I recline the leather seat all the way back. It's almost as comfy as a bed. If I could get a spare key, I'd sleep in here instead of the *kongsi*.

"Where have you been?" he asks.

"None of your business."

"You're gone a lot. What's going on?" He stops at a light and turns to me with a frown. "You seeing someone?"

"Still none of your business." Yeah, with a pillow and a blanket, this would be perfect. Too bad Mike would never go for it.

"Cat, this is serious. You can't date outsiders."

"You do."

"That's different."

"How's it different, Mr. Double-Standard?"

"I'm playing around. I'm not going to marry any of those girls."

I pull the seat upright. "Are you really going to marry Head Elder's daughter? I mean, it's the 1990s, not the 1890s. You should be able to marry whoever you want."

"The Crossroads exist outside of time, Cat. You know that. We don't live by the rules of the world. We live by our own laws, and according to the laws of our clan, marriages are arranged."

"So, I have to marry some random dude picked out for me?"

"No." He raises his voice as he says this. "I won't let that happen to you. I'll make sure you marry a good man."

I roll my eyes. "Gee, thanks."

"Are you seeing someone?"

"No. Unlike you, I'm not a player." I don't want him or anyone to know I'm at the church. That's my sanctuary. Where else would I be? "I don't want to be home. I hate it there. I go to the library or, I don't know, walk around. Whatever."

His face softens. "I'm sorry Mother is being such a bitch to you. I told her to stop calling you The Girl. "

I shrug. Since I hate Tiffany, I don't care what she thinks or says about me.

"And that it's wrong to forbid you to attend George's wedding banquet."

"Like I want to be there."

"Yeah, I don't want to go either. It's disrespectful. Mother should've waited until we had time to mourn."

I don't tell him that Tiffany purposely said in my presence, *"I'm not halting my son's wedding over the death of a mere concubine. She's nothing to him or me."*

"You know I loved Meghan." His use of my mother's name makes me stiffen. "I love her and I miss her. I always wished she was my real mother."

Then why won't you tell me how she died? That question divides us like an invisible wall. Things will never be okay between us until he answers and he knows it. There's an awkward silence that he attempts to fill with words. "Want to know who we're picking up at the airport?"

I sigh as I say, "Who?"

He grins. "None of your business."

"Be that way," I mutter.

I stare at the bay as we drive down Highway 101. The wind is making white caps appear on the surface as the water churns and laps on the rocky shore. I wish I could talk to Mike and tell him everything I'm feeling. My nose starts tingling as I realize I've barely talked to anyone, except Sylvia. She waylaid me again a couple of days ago. "By the way, that chick, Sylvia, she keeps bugging me, saying she's supposed to marry you."

Mike smirks. "Yeah. She's into me. She talks like we were dating and I broke her heart. I don't even know her."

I scoff. What a weirdo. "Well, she asked me to talk to you, but I don't know what I'm supposed to say."

"Ignore her. I mean, I do feel kinda sorry for her. I wouldn't want to marry George."

"Yeah, me neither. Or you. You're both pretty much the worst."

"Got that right. I don't know which of us is a bigger asshole." His smile fades. "Chicks dig assholes. I don't know why, but they do. Don't be that way, okay? Don't waste yourself on some jerk."

"A jerk like you? No way."

I lean forward and turn on the radio. Gangsta's Paradise comes blasting out. I love that song so much! Mike side-eyes me as I start singing along about the tragic life of being a gangsta and having to hustle, so I sing even louder.

Then it hits me. For the first time since Mom died, I feel happy. It feels so strange. Forbidden. Like I'm disrespecting her. At the same time, it feels good, as if there's a light at the end of the tunnel of my misery. Maybe that's why Mike had me come along. He knew I needed to get away. He can be thoughtful sometimes.

We get to SFO and walk through the metal detector at the security checkpoint before heading to the gate. I ask, "Who are we picking up?"

His smirk returns. "You'll see."

"Just tell me."

"Not with that attitude."

We get to the gate and I'm standing there, arms crossed, fuming. Then I look at the sign above the gate agent's desk to see where the plane is coming from.

Seattle.

I gasp as my heart starts pounding. I turn to Mike and he's grinning, so I elbow him in the ribs. "Why didn't you tell me it was Roy?"

His grin gets bigger.

"What's he doing here?"

"Helping me not go crazy during all this wedding bullshit.

That's the unofficial reason. The official reason is he's representing the Seattle *kongsi* at the banquet."

"But the banquet's in August."

"So what? I'm the Dragon Son's Heir. If I want someone to come, they come."

My nose wrinkles. I don't like how arrogant Mike is. I mean, both Mike and George are arrogant, but George is more spoiled from being raised by Tiffany. Mike, though, he thinks he's hot shit and Dad's to blame. I've heard the stories. I know that back in the day, Dad thought he was hot shit, too.

Passengers start coming through the gate. I'm practically vibrating and I feel stupid about feeling so excited. 'Heart skipped a beat' sounds so cliché, but that's exactly what my heart does when I see Roy. Tall, dark, and handsome is also a cliché, but that's him all over, even though he's got this lock of hair that always sticks up from the side of his head. It makes him look goofy and more like my brother's best friend than the guy I'm totally crazy about. He's wearing loose fitting jeans and a black T-shirt that shows his muscular frame, and has headphones hanging around his neck. Such a contrast to Mike in his fitted jeans and polo shirt.

"You look good," says my brother as they shake hands.

"You don't," replies Roy. "Been slacking off?"

"Mother has me going to parties almost every night. I haven't worked out since we got back from London. That's why I need you here, man. To kick my ass back into shape."

Roy turns to me and his grin becomes something warmer. "Hey, Cat."

"Hey." My mind goes blank. I reach for something, anything. "Um, how was your flight?" Ugh! Isn't that something you say when you're, like, fifty years old?

He shrugs. "All right." He pats the Walkman strapped to his belt. "Glad I had this."

Mike also reaches for his belt, but it's to pull out his pager. He squints at the screen before saying, "Hang on. I have to make a call." He heads for a bank of pay phones at the front of the terminal.

Roy and I follow slowly behind, the wheels of Roy's suitcase squeaking as he tugs it along. I glance back. Looks like he packed light.

"Aren't you going to the wedding banquet?" I ask.

"Yeah."

"No suit?"

He shrugs. "Apparently, I'm an usher, even though no one asked me. Anyway, Mike said a suit will be provided." We walk in silence for a bit. He takes a breath before saying, "Cat, I'm so sorry about your mom. She was awesome. I really liked her."

I stop and take a deep breath. Finally, someone says the right thing about Mom. People are rushing past us, to and from their gates, but for a brief moment I feel like we're the only two people in the airport. I clear my throat before whispering, "Thanks. She liked you, too."

He opens his mouth, but has to wait as an announcement about a cancelled flight blares from the speakers. He shuffles awkwardly and then says too loudly, "Is there anything I can do?"

Be on my side. Make Mike tell me what happened to my mother. Make Dad stop drinking. Kick Tiffany and Sylvia out of the *kongsi*. I shake my head. "Thanks."

Mike hangs up the phone and comes sauntering over, pulling his wallet from his pocket. "Something came up. I gotta go." He winks at Roy before pushing a hundred-dollar bill into his hand. "Get my sister home. I'll see you later." He strolls away toward the parking garage.

My jaw drops. What an asshole. A hypocrite. Telling me to stay away from outsiders and then ditching me and his best friend at the airport while he heads out for a booty call. I turn to Roy. His arms are folded and he's shaking his head.

"I can't believe him," I say, waiting, hoping that Roy won't defend him.

He stares after my brother with troubled eyes. "Something's going on with Mike. He's in over his head with something, but he won't tell me what. That's the real reason he wants me here, but whatever it is, I don't think I'm enough to stop him."

The anger clutching my chest sharpens to fear. What could Mike be doing that's getting him in trouble? Drugs? Gambling? Acting like a gangster, the way Dad used to do? Whatever it is, how can I help him when I can't even help myself?

Friend

There's a knock on my bedroom door. A hesitant tap followed by an insistent rap. I roll my eyes because I know who it is. Even her knock sounds passive-aggressive.

"Yeah"? I say loudly.

"It's me."

"Yeah?"

"Um. I have to show you."

"No, you don't."

"Please. I have to or she'll..."

"I don't care."

Sylvia takes that as permission and comes barging in. I grab my journal and start writing so I don't have to look at her.

Dear Mom,

Things I've learned that you never bothered telling me: Tiffany belongs to one of the families who control our clan's finances and that, unlike the rest of us, they socialize and do business with outsiders so they can grow the clan's wealth. That's the whole reason Dad couldn't just divorce her and get it over with. That's why he made you his Second Wife, as if that's even all right. Why did you go along with that? You were too good for Dad. You should've dumped him.

There's a huff of frustration followed by a whine. "I don't like doing this, you know. She makes me do it."

Sylvia belongs to one of those families, too. George told me that's why he has to marry her and that he's really sorry.

"Ca-aht! You have to look."

Tiffany decided that Mike, George and Sylvia need to be introduced to San Francisco society. That means she and Sylvia are constantly shopping for new clothes and getting their hair and nails done for dinner parties and events. Whenever they go out, Tiffany makes Sylvia come to my room and show me her new dress, a different one each time.

"Please, look at me, Cat." Sylvia moves closer to my bed and whispers, "I have to tell you something. It's important."

I look up. She's wearing a shiny pink satin cocktail dress with a low neck and a high skirt. Diamonds glitter at her ears, throat and wrists. Her hair is swept into one of those updos with the long strands framing her face. She chews her bright red lip and shifts on her shiny, three-inch heels, waiting for a compliment that won't come.

TACKY

"What are you writing?"

"None of your business."

TACKY HO!

"I wish you'd let me be your friend."

Pain spreads across my chest. I had friends in high school. Outsiders who can't know about the Crossroads or the Two Dragon Clan. I haven't spoken to any of them since Mom died. I know some girls in our clan, but they're not friends. I could never figure out why. I thought maybe it was because I'm the Dragon Son's daughter and they were jealous or something. Now I know. It's because I'm the daughter of the Dragon Son's concubine and tainted with scandal.

"I don't trust you." Or anyone.

"I don't blame you. Maybe this will help." She glances over her shoulder and leans a little closer. "Me, Mike and George are going to leave the party early. We're going to a bar and we want you and Roy to join us there."

I'm stir crazy enough that this sounds like a good idea. I set down my journal and scoot forward. "A bar? How can I get in?"

"Aren't you eighteen?"

"Yeah. You have to be twenty-one to drink here."

"Really? I don't know, then. The bar at the Mark Hopkins Hotel. It's called Top of the Mark. I think Mike would've mentioned if it was going to be a problem."

"If it's also a restaurant, I can go there."

"What strange laws you have here. Anyway, we're meeting at nine. Mike set it up so you and Roy are going out at seven."

I glance at the clock. It's almost 6:30. "Going out? Where?"

"Isn't that for Roy to decide?" She looks me up and down, from my ratty gym shorts to my grungy Pearl Jam T-shirt. "Mike says the Top of the Mark is posh, so dress like an adult."

My mouth drops open as she spins on her shiny heels and leaves my room. If she thinks I'm going to dress like some tacky ass ho, she's got another thing coming.

I leave on my Pearl Jam shirt, pull on a pair of shredded jeans, and tie a plaid flannel shirt around my waist. Then I twist my hair into double buns on either side of my head and rim my eyes with black eyeliner. This was how I dressed for school. Mike would tease me and call me Punk Rock Minnie Mouse. Like I cared what he thinks. As I stare at myself in the mirror, though, I realize I'm about to go out with Roy, and I do care what he thinks, but why? Since he's been here, he's treated me like always, like Mike's little sister. He even let Mike set up a date for us, so his opinion of my appearance doesn't matter, right?

Still, my heart starts pounding as I sit on the top stair and lace up my high-top sneakers. This is going to seal the deal. He'll never see me as anything other than a grubby kid and that's for the best. Right.

I clomp down the stairs and Roy's waiting for me in the lobby. He's wearing jeans, a black T-shirt, and a flannel shirt, like he didn't get the memo about the posh. Or didn't care. I'm kind of loving him for it and that's not good.

"Hi," I say and hate myself for sounding breathless with a single word.

"Hi." His deep voice has a rumble that makes goosebumps appear on my arms.

I pull on my flannel shirt so he doesn't see. "Yeah, so..."

"Yeah." He grins. I'm next to him now and his aftershave has this musky smell that's making my head spin.

What the hell is wrong with me?

"Are you hungry?" he asks. I nod. "How does pizza sound?"

My mouth waters. I've been subsisting on ramen and coffee for almost a month. Tiffany hired a chef and the smell of his cooking wafts upstairs. I'm never invited to join "the family" for any meals. At first, she sent plates upstairs for her husband. Not me. This was made very clear. Since Dad is never here, I would take the plate and dump the contents into the garbage disposal. I got this weird thrill at the sound of Tiffany's food being ground into sewage. Sometimes, though, the food looked and smelled so good, I had to chew my lip and force my hand as my stomach grumbled. I would rather die of starvation than eat anything from that bitch.

As we leave the *kongsi* and head downhill toward the heart of Chinatown, I keep my arms folded and about two feet distance between us. This is so damn awkward. I don't know what to say.

"Anyplace you like to go?" asks Roy. I shake my head. "There's this place in North Beach that sells pizza by the slice. It's really good, but kind of a dive."

I try to smile, but my nerves are jacked up. My stomach is squeezing from something other than hunger. I thought I'd welcome a chance to get out, but this was a bad idea. I don't want to be anyone's pity date.

"Are you all right?"

"No." I stop and turn to face him. "Mike's trying to set us up, right? Why are you going along with it?"

His eyes widen and he looks a lot younger, closer to my age. His shoulders lift in a tight shrug. "I guess because I like you and I want to hang out with you. What about you?"

"What about me?"

"Yeah, why are you going along with it?"

I'm not ready to admit I like Roy, especially not to his face. I look down. "I dunno. To get out of the house and because pizza sounds really good."

"Then, let's do it." Despite being so handsome, he's got this goofy, toothy grin. I can't help but smile back.

"Yeah, okay, but that whole Top of the Mark thing stinks. Whose idea was it anyway?"

"Sylvia's, and Mike and George got sucked into it. At least, that's what Mike told me."

I roll my eyes. Okay, now it all makes sense. Sylvia is trying to get points with Mike by helping set us up. I'm not going to be part of her stupid scheme. I pull my pager from my pocket. "I'm telling Mike I'm not going. Are you still going?"

He shakes his head. "Not my kind of place."

My eyes narrow as I glare at Mike's name. I shove the pager back in my pocket. "You know what? I'm not going to tell him. Let's just ditch them."

That grin returns and lights up his eyes. He must be sick of them and their drama, too. As we continue walking, my arms are still folded, but I'm next to Roy now, and breathing much easier. I feel like a weight's been lifted off me. Maybe this won't be such a bad evening after all.

We pass through Chinatown and cross Columbus Avenue to North Beach, the city's Italian neighborhood. It's just as touristy as Chinatown, but with fewer souvenir stores and a lot more bars. Although it's still light out, people are dressed for night and there's an energetic hum in the air as if the whole place is about to become one big party. It makes me feel giddy and up for anything.

The Ramones are blaring from the speakers as we enter Golden Boy Pizza. It's dark and narrow and looks more like a warehouse with its aluminum siding walls and roof. Nearly all surfaces are covered with band stickers. The pizza is served from sheets sitting on display in the front window. There are no tables, just two long bars with stools. The place is packed, but as Roy is placing our order, a couple gets up to leave and I snag their seats. As I sit, glancing around, my leg resting on the other stool, I wonder how I never knew such a perfect place existed.

Roy arrives with the food and I concentrate on devouring a huge slice of pepperoni pizza, washing it down with a glass of root beer. I don't think anything has ever tasted so good. I slow down on my second piece because I don't want to go home too soon. Roy is still on his first slice. He's sipping his beer and though his long limbs are arranged casually, I know from his gaze that he's checking out the crowd for danger, though what danger could we be in here?

I catch a look at the label on his bottle and I laugh and point. His face becomes quizzical. I lean closer so he can hear me above the noise. "Arrogant Bastard?"

He grins. "It's a craft beer. It's pretty good."

"Is it named after Mike?"

He holds out his bottle so we can both see the arrogant devil printed on the label. "Yeah, looks just like him."

Sharing a laugh at Mike's expense feels really good. I take a bite of my second slice. Mmm. Crispy pepperoni. So good. I lean in close again. "How did you find this place?"

"Mike's gone most evenings, so I wander around. Sometimes, I go into the clubs and check out the bands."

"What kind of bands?"

"I like roots music, so mostly R&B. I saw a zydeco band last week that was pretty hot."

"What's zydeco?"

"Do you know what Cajun music is?"

I shake my head.

"Zydeco, Cajun, and Creole music all have their roots in Louisiana. They're similar, but not identical. I guess the best way to describe it is country western and French folk music mixed with rock and R&B."

"That sounds cool." Way better than sitting at home and staring at four walls, wishing I was anywhere else. Maybe he'll take me with him next time, though the thought of asking him makes my stomach flutter.

"You like grunge music?" he asks.

I shrug. "Some, like Pearl Jam, obviously, but I also like some hip hop. I like all kinds of music."

"You should come to Seattle."

"Why? Are you going to tell me you saw Pearl Jam play in some small club back in the day?"

He grins. "And Nirvana."

I sigh. Four years doesn't seem like much, but right now it feels like a canyon between us.

He takes a sip of his Arrogant Bastard. "Seattle's cool, but it's hard to be part of a scene and in the Two Dragon Clan at the same time. I had to sneak out to see shows. Then my dad caught me and that was the end of the grunge scene for me."

"Do you think you're going to take over from your dad someday?"

"I'm supposed to, but, I dunno." He gives a sideways grin. "I have this dream."

"Tell it!"

"You can't tell anyone. Not even Mike."

"On my honor," I lift my hand.

He lifts an eyebrow. "It's not that serious. Anyway, you know how Portland doesn't have any Two Dragon Clan presence?"

I don't, but I nod anyway.

"I thought I'd offer to set up shop there. Open a *kongsi* and be the Big Brother. Except the *kongsi* would be fronted by a blues bar and I'd be the owner, and book all the bands. The perfect cover." He tips his beer through his grin.

"That's a great idea! You should totally do it." And I would totally join him.

Wait.

Where did that come from? I have feelings for Roy, but not strong enough for that, right? I munch on my pizza, trying to chew those thoughts away.

Roy sets down his bottle and does another of those casual sweeping glances of the place. Then he leans toward me, but as he starts to speak, the servers behind the bar begin whooping it up. They crank up the volume and House of Pain's "Jump Around" blasts from the speakers. A rowdy bunch at the front of the restaurant slide off their stools and start jumping and shouting as they punch their fists in the air. I start moving in time to the beat. This place is so much better than some ritzy bar. I could spend the whole night here.

Roy cups his hand to my ear. I stiffen as I feel breath soft on my cheek. He still has to almost shout. "We're being watched."

I spin around so we're facing each other. Did I hear that right? I almost-shout back, "Watched? By who?" I start looking around.

He touches my shoulder to stop me before cupping my ear again. "There's a guy in a black and gold tracksuit near the door. He's been following us since Chinatown. He came in, bought a slice, and left, so I thought maybe I was wrong. Then he came back about ten minutes ago. He's been standing there watching us ever since."

"Are you sure? Why would anyone be following us?"

"I don't know." He pauses. "Would your stepmother hire someone to follow you and see where you go?"

"She's not my stepmother and no, she doesn't give a damn what I do." Or does she? Maybe she's trying to find something damaging on me so she can kick me out of the clan. A shiver runs down my spine. I need to know. "What should we do?"

"Turn the tables. Follow him and see where he goes."

"How do we do that?"

Roy's mouth crimps. He gets this look in his eyes, like a hunter about to go after prey. "Easy. We look at him."

Lover

I crane my neck to peer around the gyrating bodies and spot the guy. He's Asian, but that doesn't mean he's with the Two Dragon Clan. San Francisco is a Crossroads fulcrum and there are lots of clans in the city. They tend to be separated by race and culture, but not all of them. He could be with the Beggar Clan, except they seldom discard their rags. He's definitely not a Shinobi. You can't see them unless they want you to.

He sees me looking at him. Our eyes meet and he looks away. His expression remains neutral as he sets down his beer and slides out the front entrance. Roy and I squeeze through the crowd in pursuit. We stand on the sidewalk and look up and down Green Street. It's twilight and the street-lights and neon signs have begun to glow, which actually makes it more difficult to see at a distance. Then I spot him in the crosswalk on Columbus Avenue. I nudge Roy and we take off running. We make it to the crosswalk as the light turns red and we sprint across to the honking of irate drivers.

As we follow him up Columbus, I'm having to trot to keep up with Roy's long legs. Should we be so obvious? It's dark enough that we can use the Shadow Skill. I need to slow him down so we can talk. This would be so much easier if we shared the Silent Speech.

Did I really just think that? I feel heat rush to my face and it's not from physical exertion.

The Silent Speech is a Two Dragon Clan skill that allows for silent communication between two people. You have to let down your barriers and open your consciousness to allow this kind of speech. It's an intimate art and involves absolute trust. Parents train their children, so I've used it with both my parents. I've also practiced it with Mike, but not George. We're not close enough for that. Close friends use Silent Speech as well, but those are usually of the same gender, like Mike and Roy. It's rare for unrelated men and women to use it, unless they're together.

Which we are not, despite whatever Mike has in mind.

We get to another crosswalk with a red light and stand well back from Tracksuit Guy, who hasn't yet turned around. That's odd. Does he really think we just sat there after we spotted him? Maybe he knows we're following him, but doesn't want us to know he knows. We need the upper hand in this.

I turn to Roy and whisper, "Shadow Skill."

He nods and juts his chin toward a closed deli. After we cross the street, we duck under its dark awning. Then he reaches out his hand. The only way we can see each other while using the Shadow Skill is if we're touching. It also involves sharing some chi, but not nearly as intimate as Silent Speech. This is no time to be shy. I take his hand and feel a little tremor as his calloused fingers wrap around mine. I take a deep breath and feel the flow of my chi, willing it to mingle with the shadows surrounding us. My hand tingles and becomes warmer as our chi meets and mingles at the contact point. I feel a sort of weightlessness as our bodies fade from view.

We slink away from the deli and stick to the shadows as we continue our pursuit, keeping the Tracksuit Guy about a block ahead of us. It's difficult having to weave and bob while holding hands past the heavy foot traffic. It isn't long before he's almost two blocks ahead. We have to use Swift Steps to follow him across Broadway without being seen. This involves accelerating our *chi* and our movement. We almost catch up to him and have to drop back. Using both these skills together expends a lot of energy. I'm not sure how much longer we can keep it up.

We're in Chinatown now, which is less crowded, but more brightly lit. We only have to use the Shadow Skill, but need to keep our hands clasped tight and allow the flow of *chi* between us to strengthen us both. The touch of his hand, the strong, steady flow of his energy is giving me feelings, like I want to be even closer to him and share even more. I wonder if he feels the same way. This isn't good. Emotions play havoc with *chi* abilities. I need to push these feelings away or we'll become visible.

We follow him up Clay Street at a steady pace until he turns into Hang Ah Alley. Interesting choice. By one accord, Roy and I slow down and creep toward the alley entrance. It's dark and empty save for a few dumpsters and laundry fluttering from the fire escapes. The only sounds we hear are the shuffle of mahjong tiles and singsong cadence of Cantonese opera coming from behind the closed doors of the family association halls. We stand completely still and wait. Tracksuit Guy steps out of a doorway and seems to be staring at us. Then he turns and continues on his way. Roy and I glance at each other. Could he see us? Are we heading for a trap? Only one way to find out. We creep along behind him, moving even more cautiously when we reach brightly-lit Chinese Playground at the end of the alley.

Tracksuit Guy turns onto Sacramento Street. We wait a few moments before taking off after him. He's running now and is almost a block away. He sprints across the street and runs into another alley.

Roy and I let go and become visible as we run after him. I'm starting to pant because this has been uphill all the way. In fact, we're close to the Mark Hopkins Hotel at the top of Nob Hill. We turn into the alley and I can see Tracksuit Guy running past a car parked at the halfway point. Even in the dark, I can tell it's a red Camaro. We stop.

"Is that Mike's car?" I whisper.

"Looks like it," Roy replies.

My heart starts racing. Why did Tracksuit Guy lead us here? Did he do something to Mike and he wants us to see? What if my brother is lying dead behind the wheel? With Swift Steps, I hurry to the car and am upon it almost at once.

The first thing I notice is that its rocking in rhythmic motion. The windows are steamy, but one of the back windows is rolled down and I can hear high-pitched female moaning and male grunting. The front passenger chair is tipped down and through that window I see Mike grinding on top of Sylvia.

My mouth drops open. I kick the car while shrieking, "You fucking asshole!"

Roy has caught up with me by now. He goes around to the passenger door, yanks it open, grabs Mike by his collar and hauls him off Sylvia.

Pain shoots through my foot. Okay, so kicking the car was stupid. I turn to hide my wince and suck in deep breaths to keep my pounding heart from exploding. At my core comes a little voice asking if I'm really that surprised. The answer is no, of course not. Mike is an asshole. A dishonorable asshole. That thought is a punch in the gut and the disappointment flooding through me hurts worse than my foot.

I turn and see the dent I made in the Camaro. Good. Roy has Mike up against the wall, demanding answers. Sylvia is leaning against the hood of the car. She straightens her skirt before bowing her head and placing a hand over her eyes. Maybe it's a trick of the shadows, but her mouth seems to twitch as if containing a smirk.

My mind starts racing. It's pretty convenient that Roy and I wound up here at just this time. What if Tracksuit Guy had been paid to lure us here? Sylvia wants to marry Mike. What better way to trap him?

Mike's defiant face shifts to concern as he glances at me. He breaks away from Roy and strides past Sylvia as if she doesn't exist. He reaches out as if he wants to hug me, but his steps slow to a halt. It must be my expression because I'm looking at him like he's the biggest piece of shit I've ever seen.

He inhales and his breath shakes out of him. "Cat. I'm... I'm so sorry. You weren't supposed to... I mean, yeah, I'm..." He runs a hand through his sticky spiky hair. "This is my fault."

"Ha!" bursts from my lips. "This isn't a broken glass, you idiot."

His eyes zigzag as he blusters, "You can't tell anyone. Promise me, on your honor, you won't tell anyone."

Really? My hands go to my hips and I shake my head. He wants me to be honorable after he's been so dishonorable. I wonder what he would do to keep my silence. I become very still, because I know exactly what he would do. Would it be dishonorable of me to require it? Probably, but at this point, I don't care.

I share the Silent Speech with Mike, but I don't want to use it. I don't want to touch his asshole mind. I whisper so Sylvia can't hear. "I won't say anything, but you have to tell me what happened to my mother."

His face stiffens. He takes a step back. "I can't. You know I can't."

I take a step forward. "You tell me or I tell George and your mother."

He rears back his head as if I'd slapped him. His eyes narrow in a hard glare. "Your room. Half an hour."

I nod.

He turns abruptly and strides toward Sylvia, barking, "Get in the car." She folds her arms and glares at him. He leans closer and says something that makes her eyes widen. Her heels click as she skitters around to the passenger side. She shoots me a pleading gaze before climbing inside.

Mike guns the engine and I jump aside as he roars out of the alley. I stare at his taillights, shaking my head. I'm trembling, my head is pounding, and my foot aches, but the worst pain is in my heart. I have no family. No one cares about me. They only care about their horrible, selfish needs.

Roy peels himself off the wall. "Hey."

I brace myself, afraid of whose side he'll take. "What'd Mike say to you?"

"Bunch of bullshit about how Sylvia seduced him. I told him that was bullshit and he needs to man up."

"What did he say?"

Roy's full lips press thin. I can see the disappointment in his eyes. "He said it would cause chaos in the clan. I told him it would cause worse chaos if this gets out without damage control. Then he said..." He takes a hesitant breath.

"What?"

"He said he's fucking Sylvia because he wants George to marry his sloppy seconds."

I feel like I'm going to puke out my pizza. Any lingering guilt I feel over forcing Mike to break his word disappears. I start limping down the alley in the direction we came in.

Roy strides ahead of me and puts his hand on my shoulder. I shrug him off, but I stop. "What?"

"How's your foot?"

"I'll live."

"You kicked the car pretty hard."

"Wish I'd kicked it harder."

A sideways smile appears briefly before he becomes serious again. "It's not worth hurting yourself. They don't deserve your pain."

That's true. I shrug. "Yeah, well, I'll suck it up."

"You shouldn't walk the hills when you're hurt. Let me help you."

"Help?" Even as I say the word, I know what he means. I don't want to let him because, at this point, I don't trust men at all. At the same time, I do want to trust one man: him. I need to because if I don't, hate and anger will poison my soul. "Yeah. Okay."

Roy kneels on the asphalt and I place my hand on his shoulder as he unties my shoe. Then he wraps his hand around my foot. It feels nice, like someone cares. Then he closes his eyes and takes a deep breath. As he exhales, his chi flows through his hands and into my foot. Warmth and healing energy spreads from my ankle to my toes. Our healing skills can't mend broken bones, but they can ease pain and open channels that have been blocked by emotion and violence. As Roy's chi flows from my foot through the rest of my body, some of my rage starts to ease as well.

That's when I feel the touch of his consciousness, and how weary and discouraged he is. It isn't fair that he's giving all his strength to me. I want to help him, too. I press my palm into his back and channel the flow of my *chi* into him.

He gives a little gasp. "Cat."

I shake my head. I want to do this, use my strength to strengthen him.

As I think this, my mind open, reaches out, and touches his. We establish contact as he says my name again using the Silent Speech, *Cat.*

Roy.

As we both stand, I can't stop myself from hugging him. His arms wrap around me and I can feel the steady beat of his heart against my chest.

I touch his mind again. *Don't hate me for what I'm about to do.*

I could never hate you.

Don't be so sure.

Honor

When we get to my room, I sit on my bed and Roy swings my desk chair around before sitting with his long arms resting on the back. Is he trying to shield himself from me? On the way home, I told him what I required of Mike for my silence. He went silent and stayed that way until we got here.

I cross my legs and rub my foot, which is still a bit tender. "You think I'm wrong?"

A deep sigh splits his grim lips. "It's not just you, Cat. I'm really disappointed in Mike. He's compromised his honor in the worst way possible. I don't think what you're asking of him will make it any worse."

That's for damn sure.

There's a short, sharp knock on the door. Before I can say anything, Mike comes striding in. He closes the door softly, though I can tell he'd rather slam it shut. He stands in the middle of the room with his arms folded, glaring at both of us. Then he takes a deep breath, exhales, and collapses beside me like a broken puppet. He rubs his palms into his eyes and moans, "Can you get me some coffee? I'm still drunk."

I want to push him off my bed, but that won't help, so I stomp off to the kitchen. I use instant coffee and a chipped mug. The good stuff isn't for assholes. When I get back to my room, Mike is sitting up and facing Roy, who's talking to him in a low voice. Whatever he said has had some kind of sobering effect on Mike, who thanks me for the coffee. Then he takes a sip.

"Jesus, Cat, what'd you make this with? Tar?" He takes another sip and grimaces. "It wasn't my idea not to tell you what happened to Meghan. You can blame Dad and George for that."

I take a deep breath, bracing myself. "Go on."

"Okay, so, we went to London because Sydney Lee was promoted from Big Brother to Head Elder of the *kongsi* and Dad had to appoint his replacement. That involves a bunch of ceremonies and banquets. One of those banquets was for the leaders of the other Crossroads clans. Mad Maud of the Beggar Clan was there. Bunch of other clans, too. I don't remember them all, except I could tell they were all sizing Dad up. Finally, the head of one of the Pakistani clans asked Dad to demonstrate the Dragon Shout. Dad said, sure, and used his power to lift the guy out of his seat and hold him against the wall before dropping him to the floor. That shut everyone down, except this one guy, the Grandmaster of the Templars. He challenged Dad to a bout."

My brow knits. Bouts are pre-challenges, a way to test strength without binding results or fatalities. I don't know much about the Templars, but they seem too small and secretive to want to take over leadership of the Crossroads.

"Dad agreed and chose swords as the weapon."

I shudder from a sudden chill because I think I know where this is going. One of Dad's favorite tricks when challenged is to accept and choose swords as the weapon. On the day of the bout, he always claims to be sick and presents Mom as his substitute. He loves sitting back and watching her take out rivals twice her size.

"The next day, we went to Temple Church to meet the Grandmaster. It was the headquarters of the Knights Templar back in the Crusader days. They were supposedly kicked out, but they actually moved their operation into the secret chambers beneath the church, and that's where we went." Mike shrugs. "It was all pretty cool at first. The Grandmaster took us on a tour and told us some of the history, like how most of the original medieval church was destroyed in the blitz during World War Two, but their chambers were deep enough to survive the bombings. Then he took us into their sacred relics room, which includes all kinds of weapons from vanquished enemies throughout the centuries. That's when George saw it." He pauses and rubs his forehead.

"Saw what?" asks Roy. The lump in my throat won't let me speak.

"A Two Dragon Clan dagger. I mean, there were a lot of daggers and other weapons, but this particular dagger was one of ours. The blade had the Two Dragon Clan stamp at the base of the hilt. The handle, though, was completely different. It had been swapped out for a handle with a red Templar cross and an embedded pearl. I have to give George credit for a good eye. I wouldn't have noticed, even though it was in the section of relics looted during the Opium Wars."

I'm not surprised since George went the scholar route in the clan rather than the warrior route, like Mike. Clan scholars are tasked with keeping our knowledge and secrets intact, and with finding the clan treasures that disappeared during the Taiping Rebellion, which coincided with the second Opium War. "So, the Templars had one of our daggers. That's not that big of a deal, is it? Unless, the pearl..."

"Exactly. George told me to touch it and I could feel its power. It was definitely one of the missing dragon pearls."

Roy and I exchange startled glances. This is big news. After Jade Dragon, the founder of the Two Dragon Clan, died in his human form and once again became a dragon, he left behind pieces of his great pearl, which is the source of his power. We still have the Yang Pearl, which the Dragon Son wears around his neck and uses to enhance his *chi* abilities. The Yin Pearl and the Wisdom Pearl were lost, along with the other treasures, during the chaos of those wars.

"What did you do?" I ask.

Mike sucks in a hard breath. "I told the little asshole to calm the hell down. That when we got a chance, we'd tell Dad and he'd negotiate with the Templars to get the dagger back. But he was all hyper and insisted that the Templars won't give it to us if they know we want it. We had to take it now, which was completely idiotic. We were surrounded by Templars who'd come to watch the bout and we couldn't possibly get out of there without a fight, which would cause war between our clans. I told him again to calm down, that we'd figure it out.

"So, we're led into this gym with mirrored walls and even more weapons. Grandmaster points out the training swords and asks Dad to take his pick. Dad gets that twinkle in his eyes and does his thing, saying he can't fight because he's sick and his wife will fight in his place."

It is his thing and the Grandmaster probably expected it and even trained for it. I hug my knees to my chest. "Mom lost the bout? Is that how she died?"

"No. It never came to that. While Meghan was choosing her weapon, a couple of Templars hauled George in. One of them was holding the dagger. They claimed he was trying to steal it. George insisted he was going to give it to Meghan to use for the bout since it's a Chinese weapon, which is obviously bull-shit since it's a dagger." Mike gives his head a contemptuous shake and mutters, "Dumb fuck." He huffs as he continues. "The Grandmaster doesn't believe that, of course, and says the penalty for stealing their sacred relics is death. He took a sword from one of the stands and started to swing it at George."

He pauses to wipe his brow. "Damn. It happened so fast. Dad was about to use the Dragon Shout to stop him, but Meghan leapt forward with her sword to deflect the Grandmaster. Thing is, she had a practice sword and he had the real thing." He closes his eyes and says through his wince, "He sliced off her arm."

I press my forehead to my knees as nausea rises from my stomach to my throat. No. Not Mom. Not like that. "Did she suffer?" I don't realize I said that aloud until Mike answers.

"She was unconscious, but still alive. Dad scooped her up and we ran out of there. The Templars didn't try stopping us. It wasn't until we got in the car that I realized George had managed to get the dagger back and bring it with him. I wanted to slit his throat with it, but I was too busy trying driving. Dad was in the back seat, trying to keep your mom from bleeding out, but it was too late. She died before we reached the hospital."

I still can't cry. I'm more angry than sad. How could Mom die like that? It can't be real. She can't be dead. Not like that. Roy sits beside me and puts his arm around me. I collapse against him, letting him hold me up because I just can't. My voice comes out in a husky whisper, "Why couldn't you tell me any of this?"

Mike sighs. "George has done a lot of research on all the pearls, and he confirmed the one on the dagger is the Wisdom Pearl. And if you remember from history, the Wisdom Pearl is the scary pearl, the one that gives the wearer the power of persuasion. Dad said it's too dangerous for anyone to wield. He ordered a new vault and put the pearl in it. Only he and I know the combination. He even decided to keep the vault in London so neither he or I can access it on a whim. He made me swear never to use it. He made both me and George swear to never tell anyone what happened to Meghan or about the pearl."

"What about the Templars?" asks Roy.

"I thought Dad might seek revenge, but he blames George more than them. All he required was their silence. He even sent the dagger back to them with a different pearl attached. If they noticed, they didn't say."

I clear my thick throat so I can speak. "Dad still sounds like Dad during all that. When did he change?"

Mike's brow furrows. "Yeah, it's weird. I mean, he was angry and grieving, but not dysfunctional. Not until we got home." He looks down. "So, I guess I should say, and you can think of me however you want, but that's why I'm messing around with Sylvia." He lifts defiant eyes. "It's my revenge against George. I don't believe his bullshit story. He was going to take that dagger and leave me, Dad, and Meghan in the hands of the Templars. He wanted all the glory of finding the missing pearl. Instead, he's going to have a wife that's already been used by his brother."

I shudder, because his words and actions are so awful, but also because I kind of understand. I want George to pay, too, but like that? And what about Sylvia? Yeah, she's a manipulative bitch, but she didn't do anything to hurt us.

"That's messed up," says Roy. "You need to cut that shit out. Seriously. Not just because it's wrong, but you're being played. You think Cat and I wound up in the alley by accident?" He tells Mike about Tracksuit Guy.

Mike shakes his head. "Doesn't surprise me one bit. She told me she's on the Pill, but I don't believe her, so I'm using a condom. She keeps trying to get me not to, but," He shrugs. "Not falling for that."

Is it really worth it, having sex with someone you don't trust? Does that add to the thrill or make the revenge sweeter? I don't ask because I don't want to know. I'm feeling sick enough already.

"Okay, I told you two the truth. Now, you have to hold up your end of the bargain and swear not to tell anyone about me and Sylvia."

Roy and I exchanged glances as our minds touch.

We have to, he says.

I know, I reply, *but it's still the worst because now we have to live with it.*

Not like he has to.

I don't know about that. From where I'm sitting, Mike looks like he's living with it just fine.

"On my honor," says Roy.

"On my honor," I croak out.

As if honor has anything to do with all this.

Mother

Dear Mom,

Now I know what happened. I don't want to be angry, but I am. My hand is shaking as I write this. How could you, Mom? George wasn't worth your life. He wouldn't have done the same for you. He left you to face the consequences. He didn't love you. His mother hates you and is happy you're dead.

Why?

Why?

WHY?

I throw the journal across the bed and sit with my arms folded tight. I'm not crying. I'm too mad for tears. Why did I think I'd find some relief or closure? I should've known from the way Dad and the twins are behaving that the truth would lead to bitter anger and more questions.

I'd feel better if I could believe that Mom had died retrieving the Wisdom Pearl. Anyone in the clan would be willing to die to recover our lost treasures. Am I a bad person that I think she wasted her life on George? Would I die to save him? Absolutely not. I had to stop myself from telling Mike to carry on with Sylvia.

I close my eyes and picture Mom. She never said anything bad about Tiffany, at least not in front of us kids. She went out of her way to make George feel at home and part of the family whenever he visited. I said he didn't love her, but maybe he did. I remember that time when he was thirteen and I overheard him begging Dad not to send him back to Hong Kong. I reach for my journal.

Did you love George? Is that why you did it? Or did you do it because you love Dad and didn't want him to lose a son? Maybe that's what makes me so angry. It's like you were thinking of them, but not me. I shouldn't have had to lose you, Mom, not for any reason, and especially not because George wanted glory. I guess there's some consolation that no one will ever know and George is covered in shame instead.

I set down the book this time and close my eyes. I picture Mom in a myriad of images: lighting the candles for my sixteenth birthday cake, helping me with calculus, exchanging a quick kiss with Dad. I inhale to capture the memory of how she smelled. I rub my hand to remember her touch. These memories are more precious than diamonds, but how long until they start to fade?

Tears leak through my closed lids as I finally start to cry.

Brother

Dear Mom,

George's wedding is tomorrow. I can't be happy for him. I'm trying to forgive him. I wonder if he'll forgive me if he ever finds out about Mike and Sylvia, and that I knew and didn't tell him. I also wonder if he'll care. He escorts Sylvia when required, but otherwise doesn't hang out with her or try to get to know her. I overheard Mike and George talking about the bachelor party tonight. From what I could tell it involves strippers and getting them both laid. Nice.

If it weren't for Roy, I wouldn't want to get married. In fact, I know I won't marry anyone but him. I know what you'd say, that I'm too young, I need to wait and meet more men. You even hinted that I didn't need to marry within the clan. I understand now you meant that, despite being the Dragon Son's daughter, I'm not a desirable wife. And that's okay. I'd rather be your daughter than be someone desirable like Sylvia.

I was worried that Roy's family won't approve of me, but he assured me they don't care about my status. Seattle is different, he said. Less formal and less attached to clan tradition. I wish I could move there right now. I'm almost tempted to transfer to a university there, but that'd be stupid. I worked too hard to give up my admission to Berkeley just because I fell in love.

I do love Roy, Mom. He's been there for me like no one else. I wish you could've gotten to know him better. You'd really like him. The real him. Not just Mike's tall, quiet friend. He's not going to the bachelor party. He's spending the evening with me, hanging around North Beach and checking out the clubs.

We haven't done much more than kiss. Roy hasn't pressured me. I think I want to do more, but when I think about sex, I remember Mike and Sylvia in the car and it's a big turn-off. I'm not so innocent that I believe sex is only about love, but I didn't know it could also be about hate. It's going to take me awhile to get over that.

Besides, Roy and I share the Silent Speech and that's more intimate. When we're in a loud and crowded place and can communicate as if there's no one else in the room, it makes me feel so much closer to him.

There's one thing that's bugging me, though. Roy is still going to the wedding banquet. I know he has to, that he's representing his family and the clan in Seattle, and all that stuff, but if he really loves me, why doesn't he stand by me and refuse to go? I didn't ask him because I'm afraid that if I do, he'll say no, he has to be there to support Mike. Which will make me face the one thing I dread most: will Roy always choose Mike over me?

Because I'm really afraid the answer is yes.

Dragon

I can't sleep. The guilt of keeping Mike and Sylvia's affair hidden is eating away at me. I know I gave my word, but is my word worth betraying my brother? Or is this my revenge against George and I'm an awful person?

I glance at the glowing red numbers on my alarm clock. It's almost 4 a.m. I suck in another deep sigh and close my eyes. This time, I drift off. I dream... I don't know what. Things that feel so real, like another life I should be living. The sound of footsteps, slammed doors, and loud voices pull me from this other life. I wake up and the noise is still there. I look again at the clock. It's 5:30. Are wedding preparations always this early?

I was going to stay in my room and ignore the whole thing, but since I can't sleep and I'm bored, I get up. I go to the kitchen, make myself a cup of coffee, and settle at the top of the stairs. I hear Tiffany barking commands like a high-pitched drill sergeant. Although outsiders aren't allowed inside the *kongsi*, she's open the door to an army of hairdressers and make-up artists. I hear the chatter of unknown female voices. They must be Sylvia's bridesmaids. Were her friends flown in or did Tiffany assign them from local influential families? The latter is more likely. I hear male voices approaching the foot of the stairs.

"Yeah, they're getting married in a goddam church," says Mike. "Can you believe it?"

"How did your mother manage to swing Grace Cathedral?" Roy's low voice makes my heart jump.

"Last minute cancellation. Plus, Mother throws money and things happen."

"Don't you have to be Christian to be married there?"

"Only one person has to be, so Sylvia lied. She's good at that."

And so are you, asshole! I want to shout down the stairwell. I don't, though, because I like sitting here. I find comfort in being where I belong, on the fringe of everything.

I get up to pour myself another cup of coffee and settle down again. Despite the extra caffeine, I start yawning and my eyelids droop. I lean my head against the wall and close my eyes. The downstairs hubbub becomes a white noise. I drift away, trying to recapture that dream. No one in my family is there. Not Mom. Not even Roy. I'm where I belong, surrounded by people who treat me like a person and not an inconvenience. I'm doing something I like, but what?

Clicking heels jar me awake. Tiffany rounds the corner, sees me, and looks right through me as she continues up the stairs, a black tuxedo crushed in her arms. She's wearing a dress that glitters so hard, it hurts. Her hair is piled atop her head in a mass of forced curls and she's wearing so much makeup, I wouldn't recognize her if I saw her on the street. The temptation to push her as she passes me is so strong, I have to sit on my hand. As she heads down the hall, I crane my neck and watch as she yanks open Dad's door, pauses for a moment, tosses in the tuxedo, and slams it shut. As she turns, her icy smile makes me shudder. Then she sees me and a martyred frown masks the smile. As she clicks past me, I cross my legs so I don't trip her.

After a few moments, Tiffany's aggrieved voice carries up from below. "I tried, I really did, but it's no use. He's too drunk to attend his son's wedding. Such a disgrace. He ran wild with that concubine, and now look at him. He can't function as a father, let alone as the Dragon Son."

I really should've pushed her.

I've had enough. This is more depressing than entertaining. I stand, but pause before heading toward my room. Should I check on Dad? It's been a few days since I've seen or even heard him. I assumed it's because I'm now sleeping through the sound of him stumbling home. If he's aware of what's happening today, it must be rough. I still love him. I don't blame him for Mom's death, but I'm so angry with him for abandoning me. I get this tingling sensation in my stomach, like I really need to check on him. My chest is tight as I tap on the door before opening it.

The room is dark and reeks of stale alcohol and unwashed clothes. Dad is sitting on the edge of the bed, taking a swig from a half-empty bottle of Jack Daniels. I don't blame him. Tiffany has that effect on people. I'm tempted to grab the bottle and take a swig myself. He sees me and wipes his mouth with his bare arm before patting the space beside him. "My Little Dragon Girl."

That's his nickname for me. The sound of it, after so long, gives me a wisp of hope. Maybe there's a chance he can come back to himself. I kick away the fallen tuxedo before perching beside him and taking away the bottle. His shaking hand offers little resistance. "Dad, you have to stop. You're killing yourself."

His bloodshot eyes fill with tears and his voice slurs. "I deserve to die. I should've died. Not your mother. She was worth ten of me. And you are worth twenty of your worthless brothers. Little Dragon Girl. Strong and brave. You should be the heir. Why shouldn't there be a Dragon Daughter?"

He reaches around his neck and takes off the Yang Pearl. The gold chain is dulled in the dark, but the pearl seems even more luminous. Then he places it around my neck.

"Dad, no," I protest. Talk about forbidden. Only the Dragon Son and his heir can wear the Yang Pearl. I start taking it off, but Dad grasps my hands.

"No. I don't want it. I don't deserve it. Neither does Mike. You keep it. Use it. Don't let your brothers have it." As he speaks, he crawls back under the bedding, covering his head so that his last words are muffled, "I love you, baby."

Does he mean me or Mom? I take a deep breath to ease the ache in my chest and say, "I love you, too, Dad."

I leave the room, taking the bottle with me. As I dump the remaining liquor down the kitchen sink, I debate whether or not to tell Mike about the Yang Pearl. Knowing him, the real him, he might jump at this chance to snatch it before Dad dies. No way I'm letting him do that. Maybe I should tell Roy. I go back to the stairway and am greeted by silence. Everyone has left to go to that farce of a wedding.

I return to my bedroom, intending to spend the morning going over my orientation documents for Berkeley, but I can't resist staring at my reflection in the mirror. The Yang Pearl gleams on my chest. Well, hell. What am I supposed to do with it? Leave it on his nightstand? Not smart. Hide it somewhere? I lift it up and feel a faint hum in my fingers that reverberates in my chest. If only Jade Dragon were here, though I don't know what good that would do. He only speaks to his descendants once a year during the Summoning Ceremony.

I squeeze the pearl into my palm, press it against my chest, and close my eyes. *Please, Jade Dragon, Ancestor, if you're out there, help my father.*

The hum in my chest spreads throughout my body, its energy making my fingers and toes tingle.

Your father can help himself, but he won't.

My eyes pop open. That voice, it spoke using the Silent Speech, but I don't know it. I feel a presence nearby, ancient, cold, scaly, surrounded by water. Not human.

Jade Dragon?

That is what you call me. The voice has a reptilian hiss.

Why are you talking to me?

You are someone different using this pearl. A female. Interesting.

Does my father talk to you like this?

No. I'm not interested in talking to him. I watch him. That's more interesting, though not lately. All he does is drink and mourn.

This can't be Jade Dragon. He's wise and strong, and aids us in our darkest hour. This presence sounds more like an impartial observer. But who else could it be? Maybe you need to ask Jade Dragon for help before he'll do anything.

Can you talk to him and tell him to stop drinking and pull himself together?

Nothing will change his fate. He will soon die.

What? No! I run to the door. Then I see what I missed when I came in. A folded piece of paper laying on the floor. It has my name on it.

You should read that, says Jade Dragon.

Why?

The presence slips away, swimming through the depths of the San Francisco Bay toward the Pacific Ocean. The power ebbs from my body, becoming once again a faint hum. Was I really talking to Jade Dragon? How is that even possible? I don't know how to use the Yang Pearl. I'm no one to him, unless maybe I'm the only one left who can do what he bids. I unfold the note.

Look under Tiffany's mattress.

I blink several times. Not what I expected. Who wrote this? Who else but Sylvia. Do I want to play her game? Do I have a choice? I go to the bathroom and find a hairpin. Most of the doors inside the *kongsi* have crappy, old locks. George showed me, years ago, how easy it is to pick them. I pause when I reach the second floor. I can feel the silence, that no one is here. Still, my stomach trembles as I creep down the hall. I head straight for the master bedroom. My breath goes shallow as I turn the knob. It's locked. I smirk as I fiddle with the hairpin and feel that satisfying click as the handle turns.

I slip inside, close the door behind me, and turn on the light because the blinds are shut. I squint, but not because of the light. The room is furnished completely different than before Tiffany moved in. Everything is gold-leafed in a fake antique European style. That's fine. I'll have the guards toss it all into the gutter after she leaves. There's a clothing rack in the middle of the room, hanging heavy with garment bags. During a Chinese wedding banquet, the bride changes her outfits at least four or five times. It figures Tiffany plans to do so as well. After all, this is really her wedding.

Instinct sends me to the far side of the bed. I bend down, grasp the gold satin cover, turn it over and lift the mattress. There is something there. A sword.

I grasp it by its plain wood scabbard and tug it out. It's long and heavy, meant for someone taller and stronger than me. It has a plain silver handle with a simple black grip. Its only decoration is the red Templar cross embossed into its pommel.

What is Tiffany doing with a Templar sword? Even as I think this, I feel it. I know it. My stomach twists on itself, becoming a hard ball. My breath comes in shaky spurts. Mom's death wasn't an accident. Tiffany paid the Templars to act as assassins.

This is the sword that killed my mother.

This sword is now my weapon and will kill my enemy.

Death

There's no way to sneak out the *kongsi* front door carrying a sword, even with a skeleton crew of security guards on duty. I could try disguising it, but what could I use that wouldn't look like something wrapped around a sword? I don't have time for such nonsense. The easiest option is going out the emergency exit on the ground floor. There's no guard, but there is an alarm, which would be a problem if I didn't know the code.

I step out to a narrow, damp walkway that seldom sees the light of day. I look up and see a security camera pointed right at me. Damn. My emotions are robbing me of common sense. I can only hope the guards aren't paying attention. I breathe deep and channel the power of the Yang Pearl.

Wow. My whole body feels energized, like I can do anything. Using the Shadow Skill, I hurry through the maze of tiny back alleys until I reach Taylor Street. Ordinarily, that would deplete my *chi*, but the Yang Pearl contains a deep reservoir of power.

Still in stealth mode, I use Swift Steps to bound up Nob Hill, all the way to Grace Cathedral. When I get there, I'm barely winded, but I'm dizzy from the rush of energy. I'm about to tip over and I tuck myself in a doorway leading to the church's lower level as I become visible. I catch my breath and peek out at the wide, round staircase leading up to the gothic marble towers of the church. A crowd of well-dressed Chinese people are standing around, talking. Is the wedding over already? I look them over, but I don't see Tiffany. She must still be inside.

Am I really going to kill her in a church?

My emotions, combined with the Yang Pearl, play havoc with my *chi*. A wave of dizziness forces me to lean against the wall and I take deep, slow breaths. If I wait too long, I'll get cold feet. I have to act without hesitation...

But what if I'm being played? What if Tiffany is using Sylvia and I'm heading into a trap? Except the last thing Tiffany wants if for me or anyone to disrupt the wedding. Sylvia. She's using me. Should I let that stop me? And what about Jade Dragon? Why would he allow me to use the Yang Pearl if not to purge this evil from our clan?

The door behind me opens. A hand reaches out and yanks me inside. It's Mike. He hauls me into a nearby classroom and shuts the door. Roy is waiting there. Both are wearing tuxedoes and looking impossibly handsome and horrible. Roy immediately steps in front of the door, blocking any chance of exit. I tug away from Mike and clutch the sword to my chest even though it's the instrument of my mother's death. Does her blood still stain the blade? My pulse is pounding in my ears and I'm hating them both. "Why aren't you at the wedding?"

"Wedding's over," says Mike. "The happy couple is taking photos inside the church. And by happy couple, I mean George and Mother."

That means I still have a chance. I glance over my shoulder, looking for another door. There isn't one. The only way to get past Mike and Roy is to use the Yang Pearl, but how do I do that without hurting them and me? To make time, I ask, "How did you know to find me?"

"A guard paged me and told me he saw you leave the *kongsi* by the emergency exit and that you were carrying a sword. Who told you?"

He knows about it. I suck in yet another sense of betrayal. "Sylvia. She left me a note. How long have you known?"

"Not long. Sylvia kept hinting that something sinister was going on and that she'd tell me only if I agreed to marry her. It's a lot worse than just your mom's death, Cat."

Like anything could be worse than that. "What do you mean?"

"The clan astrologer told Head Elder that the next born Dragon Son will be the new family dragon. Mother wants power over that dragon, but she won't get it through me. She hired the Templars to kill Meghan. George didn't know and it was just a coincidence that he saw the dagger and realized it held the Wisdom Pearl. The Templars used that coincidence to make Meghan's death look accidental. Afterward, they gave Mother the sword that killed her and she took it to a Taoist sorcerer who placed a curse on it."

I make a scoffing sound. Mike reaches out and I back away. He rolls his eyes. "Fine. Pull out the sword and you'll see."

I look from him to Roy to see if they'll make any sudden move. Then I tug on the handle. As the blade comes out of the sheath, I see a yellow slip of paper taped below the hilt, scrawled with twisted talismanic characters. My arm starts tingling. Something is crawling up my hand. A centipede. Centipedes. Hundreds of tiny ones crawling out of the hilt. I let go of the sword, frantically shaking and swatting my hand.

The sword falls to the floor with a clank. I stare at it, my motions slowing to a stop. There aren't any centipedes. The tingling sensation has already gone.

Roy is beside me. "Are you all right?"

I shake my head and look at Mike with wide eyes. "What kind of curse?"

"Sylvia told me that every night, Mother lays on her bed, holding the sword, and chanting a spell. As long as she keeps doing that, it will drive Dad insane and slowly kill him."

I gasp. "Why didn't you get rid of it and her?"

"Because there's more. After Dad dies, Mom will claim that George and I were switched at birth. That he's the true Dragon Son and I'm an imposter. You and I will be taken prisoner and then disappear. She'll claim we escaped, but…" He pauses. A chill tingles through me. "Yeah. Then she'll rule the clan through George. I decided to play the long game so she wouldn't get suspicious and act too soon."

"When did Sylvia tell you?"

"Last week. She's been playing Mother's minion this whole time, gaining her trust. I guess she thinks she's going to come out on top, no matter what happens."

"But you promised to marry her if she told you everything."

He shrugs. "I played her, like she's been playing us, all the way until this morning. I told her I won't marry her, but I also won't force her to marry George. That if she wants to leave, go right ahead. I won't let anyone stop her. But if she tells anyone what happened between us, I'll make her life a living hell. She made the choice to go ahead and marry our piece of shit brother. That's on her."

That's why Sylvia shoved the note under my door. I was her last hope and I arrived too late. Good. My voice shakes as I ask, "What about your mother? You're going to let her walk away?"

"My mother." He gives a humorless laugh. "As if she was ever that to me. No, she'll pay for her crimes."

"How?"

"After the wedding, she's heading back to Hong Kong with George and Sylvia to stage her coup. I hired a Five Venom practitioner. She'll be dead before the plane lands."

Roy sucks in a hard breath. "She's still your mother. Are you sure you want to kill her? Can't you just banish her?"

"There's always a price to be paid for using evil sorcery." Mike's eyes go ice cold. "And for treason. I can't let her live."

Death by poison. The Five Venoms know what they're doing. It'll probably look like she died in her sleep. As if that's anywhere near punishment enough. I want her to know she's failed and lost everything.

The power of the Yang Pearl glows in my chest. I need to do

something, but what? I reach out to that scaly presence, now frolicking in the waves off the San Mateo coast. *What can I do?*

Jade Dragon pauses. I feel his gaze on our tragic scenario and sense his renewed interest. *You can use my power, but it won't be wise.*

Will it kill me?

It could. Or kill something inside you.

There's not much left to kill. What do I need to do?

Do what you need to do. Let the pearl's energy guide you.

The glow of power extends to my arm. I reach down and pick up the sword, ripping off the evil talisman.

"Cat, don't," says Roy as he and Mike come toward me.

Using the power of the pearl, I push with my free hand and leave it outstretched, forcing them against the wall and holding them there. I start trembling and my breath shakes because it's taking nearly all my energy to do just that.

I delve deeper into the pearl and feel its whirling yang energy. I hold the sword upside down, feeling the residue of Tiffany's evil energy still present in the hilt. I focus on that energy and use the power of the pearl to send it back to her. I connect with her. She's standing in front of the church altar, posing like a queen between George and Sylvia. The photographer tells her to hold the pose, but she's startled and starts skittering away. She knows it's me wrapping her own evil magic around her heart and squeezing. She falls.

I start to fall. Roy catches me as Mike grabs the sword away. Then, nothing.

When I wake up, I'm on the floor of the classroom, cradled in Roy's arms. Mike is gone and so is the sword. I reach around my neck, though I already know. I feel the lack of the glowing power of the Yang Pearl. I look into Roy's eyes and see the turbulence of worry and anger, and maybe, just maybe, still some love. I try reaching out with the Silent Speech, but he won't let me in.

"Did I kill her?" I ask.

"Yes."

"Do you hate me?"

"No." He blinks as he says this.

I still love him. That hasn't died. But can our love, or any love, survive all these terrible things that must remain hidden?

The story continues in Fake: Dragons of the Crossroads Book 1. Michael Lau's son, Paul, is poised to become the next Dragon Son until murder slices through his family. Fleeing from traitors desperate to control him, Paul changes his name and takes to the streets, intent on delivering fiery justice. Then he meets Penny Sparrow, a girl from a rival clan, who's on her own quest for vengeance. The two teens form an unlikely alliance, but will their growing love seal their doom?

To find out more about Dragons of the Crossroads and to purchase more books in the series, please go to loriwriter.com.

Heartfelt thanks to Jennifer Gagliardi, my editor and friend.

About the Author

Lori Saltis left her heart in San Francisco. She goes to visit it whenever she can afford the bridge toll. She's been an indie author since 2016. She's very passionate about the themes of alienation and found family. Her favorite genre is fantasy because who doesn't want to believe they'll look up in the sky one day and see a dragon?

To find out more about the world of the Crossroads, check out her website loriwriter.com.